FROM

LAST

TO

FIRST

ROBERT S SMITH

To order additional copies of this book, contact:
Xlibris
844-714-8691
www.Xlibris.com
Orders@Xlibris.com

ISBN: Softcover   978-1-6698-6652-7
        EBook   978-1-6698-6651-0

Print information available on the last page

Rev. date: 02/09/2023

PREFACE

This book mainly focuses on my years running track, from early competition in the '70s to the early '80s. In 1981, I was part of an exciting distance-medley-relay team, this team jocking back and forth and winning the prized golden watch. The year 1982 would dawn the record-breaking sprint medley team. We were ranked last or fifteenth. Our squad would win the race placing us for a short time first in the nation. I used nicknames for my childhood friends. I feel this book will also be reminiscent of rock and roll and restaurants we had during that time.

ACKNOWLEDGMENTS

A special thanks to my mother for keeping such good track pictures and film. Without them, this book would not be written.

A heartfelt thanks to my wife who put up with me staying up all night and sleeping all day to write and to my daughter K for all the help with the computer.

Also to my OHS and El Modena track squads, thanks for the encouragement.

Thanks to Susan Mitchell for her Lost Cause memories.

Thanks to Richard Dunn for his help.

Thanks to everyone who took the time to talk to me. God knows I had many conversations with members of the distance medley and sprint medleys.

Track mate Mike S., who shares symptoms of our common condition, continues to check on me.

To the El Modena coach with the kind smirk and straw hat, RIP, 1938–2011.

To our sprinter coach, with his humor and hands-on training. I think he, at the age of fifty-three, was faster than us. I will always remember your grin and the fun we had. He passed on October 28, 2013.

To our cross-country/track coach who helped us get into the best invitationals and run against some of the best runners in the state.

I would like to say a special thanks to the sprinters of my track squad: to the Blur; to the Comedian for our talks, texts, and advice on writing; to the Humble Star; and to the 880 Star for their patience while I continued to text them and for still supporting me.

To my longtime friend, writer Richard D., for his advice on publishing.

A very special thanks to Scott T. of the El Modena cross-country team. He continues to keep the memories alive through the web and his willingness to help in any way he can.

Thanks to Craig S. for his help too.

Robert S. Smith

CHAPTER

My First Race

In 1969, my only escape was listening to music from groups such as Badfinger, Classics IV, The Grassroots, Three Dog Night, Tommy James and The Shondells, Vanity Fare, and The Youngbloods. I was six years old, and my family moved several times before settling into my final grammar school at Lampson Elementary School in Garden Grove, California, in late 1970. It has been unclear to me whether it was really in Garden Grove and just in Orange Unified School District. The first school was in Bakersfield, and I remember I suffered some drama from a teacher who would tape my mouth closed and hit my fingers with a ruler. We then moved to Garden Grove, California, near my mother's side of the family. I am now seven. It was there I started school at Lincoln Elementary, and this is where I would have my first track race. It was on grass. Ironically, I remember nothing about that school but this race. It was either a 75-yard or 100-yard dash. I do remember even then I was faster than the other kids I knew at that time. My hope was to get the larger first-place trophy rather than the four-inch second- or third-place one. So on the day of the race, it was like most sunny days in California, and there were eight of us who lined up for this race. The gun goes off, and I am probably 10 yards ahead of everyone, and then I see a flat rock under the grass, but it is too late. I trip and fall, and the runners pass me toward the finish line. They are probably a good 20 yards ahead, but I bolted up to catch them. I caught up to all but the winner and had to settle for a second-place finish.

In the years 1970–1973, the music of the bands like Chicago, Free, Grand Funk, Focus, Steeling Dan, and The Rolling Stones, to name a few, would influence me to run. We spent a very short time living near Mom's side of the family. We moved yet again. This time to the Georgetown apartments in Garden Grove, California. I was still in first grade but would also spend part of my second grade there. Many kids my age and older from Lampson Elementary school would live there. My best friend at the time was a kid a couple of years older. He was into magic, and we became very good friends. We once stayed up for over two days straight practicing tricks and going to a magic show. But he too would move away, and the kids left, I was not very close with. I remember I was a smaller child than the other kids. I am eight now, and I would try out for tackle football. I was primarily used for what they called "the rabbit." This is where I would sprint down the sideline while the team tried to tackle me. However, I was not big enough to make the team and was cut from the roster.

One day at the Georgetown apartments, I found a tennis ball on the grass and started bouncing it against a wall over at another apartment balcony. A neighbor kid about three years older named Greg said that was his ball and to give him the ball or he was going to kick my ass. I was, indeed, afraid of him, but I felt he was far enough away to get away with it. I threw the ball again, but it accidently got stuck in someone else's apartment balcony, and he charged toward me, screaming profanities. I got to the front of my apartment, and the door was locked. I turned around and began striking the door for my mother to open the door, yelling, "Mom! Mom!"

I turned around, facing Greg, and my mom had opened the door as I clenched my fist. The momentum had made me fall back, but it had given me a powerful punch, and I kid you not, Greg went flying through the air. I remained in fear of him, but he never bothered me again, and I have to admit I felt rather proud of the once-in-a-lifetime incident.

CHAPTER 2

We Move Again

Well, for our next move, I began the third grade, and I am nine years old. This is another apartment in a fourplex unit on Allard Street, closer to Lampson Elementary School. It was in Garden Grove, at the dividing line. If I crossed the street, I would be in the Garden Grove School District. As it stood, I was still in the Orange School District and living in the city of Garden Grove. It is now a couple of years spent with no memorable athletics to speak of, except maybe tetherball and four square. The school was divided in half, where the kids grades 1–3 were closest to the office, and there was a burn line in the grass we were not to cross until the fourth grade. My mother finds a small house she wants to rent just down the street on Anzio. My mother would take various jobs like working for Kawasaki and Tab Answering Service to support us, which left me a latchkey child for a while before she would meet my soon-to-be stepfather.

In those days, most of the schoolkids would know to be home before the streetlights came on and it was dark. My mom liked to jokingly say, "Be home before dark or your ass is grass, and I am the lawnmower."

I believe she had learned to say that from my stepfather.

I never wanted to actually test that theory, so I learned many times over the years to sprint home if it was close to dark.

3

CHAPTER

Running becomes a Metaphor

Do you remember, in chapter 1, I said I was into magic before? One day, as I have done many times before, I walked to 7-Eleven. Sometimes it would be by skateboarding. On this day, I walked down the side of apartments to get to a brick wall that was broken so you could walk through it. It was a shortcut to a small strip mall of stores, such as Photomat, 7-Eleven, The Coachman Bar, Pizza Grotto, and the Blessed Basket Broaster. If I was riding a skateboard, it would be in the Oakwood apartments as you could ride underneath the parking structure or the second floor and end on the other side. At 7-Eleven, I would meet a man who noticed me buying some sort of magic trick and also getting another one from the bottom of my Slurpee cup. Coke-and-cherry Slurpees were the best. They were larger, tastier, and a lot less expensive in those days. The man came up to me and said, "Oh, you are into magic?"

He then said he had lots of tricks at his place, and he could show me how to do them. He stated he lived at the Oakwood apartments. I am a naive nine-year-old and agree to visit. He maybe showed me a couple of tricks, and then he handcuffed me. Though he did not rape me, he laughed for a couple of hours as I squirmed for fear for my life. He finally unhandcuffed me, and this was one of the many times I ran out of fear to my home. I told my parents what had happened. They asked where he lived, and since I could not remember the exact apartment, the incident was not reported to the police. My parents said it's over. I do not remember being comforted but told by my mother. My mother had said, "I guess you'll know better next time."

I went with friends for a time until I was no longer afraid to go to 7-Eleven or the Pizza Grotto on my own. My mother always liked to say, "Whatever doesn't kill you makes you stronger."

I still hate that quote.

There were lots of instances of turmoil at home, and let's just say my parents divorced over many issues. I probably should mention my dad was eighteen and my mom was sixteen when they originally married. This would kind of play into my awkward feelings of not being sure who my actual cousins were later.

CHAPTER

CHAPTER

I Develop Type 1 Diabetes

My mother remarries, and shortly afterward, I get some unusual signs.

I am constantly in need to urinate and am extremely hungry and thirsty all the time. I would beg for more to eat and more to drink. Even though at times I would eat like two sandwiches, fries, fruit dessert, and more, I would want more to eat as my mom would exclaim, "You can't be hungry!"

The kicker was, instead of gaining weight, I was drastically losing it. I first went to a urologist named Dr. Cohen, who thought I had some possible urinary tract infection. I am ten to ten and a half years old now. He states he will run some tests and I will need only one shot. However, he would stick one needle down the center of my penis, and well, guys, that is a pain I never will forget. I come out on a gurney, where they put IVs in each arm, and well, that is all I luckily remember for that day. I then peed blood with burning for what I think was at least a week. This urologist said he does not know what is wrong with me. My mother said we were referred to an endocrinologist. It was there my mother was told how lucky I was. My sugar was 1,500, and I had maybe two days to live. I always thought you would be dead at six hundred or seven hundred, who knows. I do know I thought I would die.

Between 1973 and 1974, my mother took me to a pediatric, Dr. Lanny Taub, who named most of my symptoms in his office located in the Orange County area. I was then transferred and treated in a hospital by renowned endocrinologist, Dr. Ann Kirschner. She had worked at Children's Hospital of Orange County (CHOC). However, I would be treated for a week at Santa Ana Tustin Community Hospital. It was located on North Tustin Avenue in Santa Ana from 1972 and later closed in 1975 over it's name, I think.

Do I dare say I actually had fun in that hospital? I am probably eleven now. I was placed on the third-floor adolescent ward. I was diagnosed with type 1 juvenile onset diabetes. There was a guy in traction, a good-looking blonde with some other disease, and maybe one or two other patients who had shorter stays. There was a game room with a pool table, a stereo, and it had various board games. Now this room had swivel doors on it, and we took to the stereo quite often. This week I stayed at this hospital, the nurses would constantly have to tell us to turn down my records. We had cranked up *Chicago's Greatest Hits* album. We also played many other artists' albums on the turntable. I can still remember laughing as the swivel doors came open and the music was heard all the way down the hall. We had played games like truth-or-dare, and it was a blast.

My father and stepfather would come in and practice saline shots to experience what it would be like for me to give insulin shots to myself. I practiced on oranges. My stepfather would play me in many games of pool and win money in which my mother would tell him to give it back and laugh. I had various jobs to get money, like working for the Orange County News as a paperboy, lawn-mowing, or collecting aluminum cans and bottles. In those days, I had to test my urine for blood sugar readings and ketones. I remember using two drops of urine mixed with water into a glass tube, which got so hot I thought it could burn through anything. The ketone test was done less often, and I did it only if the urine turned orange, proving my sugar was very high. I always dreaded it turning orange as this meant you were high and needed a shot of insulin, and if it was blue in color, well, good. Now I get a snack. Now my life would be altered.

I believe diabetes would have an effect on running. Some may say, "Well, since you have to eat healthy, so maybe it was an advantage?"

I did not eat as well as I should have, so I assure it was not. Diabetes is a story unto itself as over 1.25 million can attest to. So here's a shout out to my brothers and sisters who must deal with this condition for the rest of their lives as a type 1 diabetics.

5

CHAPTER

The Olympian

In 1974, there was a very famous female track star who attended Orange High School in Orange, California. She held several world records. She held every U.S. record from the 800 to the 10,000 meters in various years. In 1968, this athlete moved from New Jersey to Garden Grove, California. I was born in Anaheim, California, but had moved to Fresno until I was six. My mom and dad had a bar called the Palm Olive. It was a biker-type bar. I was told even the hell's angels had gone there. I still seem to remember a cover band playing The Doors music. I was scared to quickly walk through there, which was rarely allowed. At the same time, my mom and dad also had a bookstore directly across the street. The bar would close because of the costly damage caused by various hooligans. The bookstore would close soon after. We then moved to Bakersfield, where we would spend a short time before moving to Garden Grove.

In 1972, I was nine, and the already-famous track/middle-distance runner was just fourteen with times already worthy of the Olympics. She was ultimately a part of the 1980, 1984,1988, and 1996 Olympic teams. I was attending Lampson Elementary and lived in Garden Grove. In the fourth grade, I had a girl in my class named Denise, who had the same last name of this very famous star athlete. She looked like this star and claimed to be her sister. I have searched for famous athletes for siblings and, at first, found nothing. Then I finally found a newspaper article of her days growing up with a brother. The star Orange High athlete moved to Garden Grove and went to Orange High, and she is only almost five years older than me. Is it a coincidence?

Ironically, I would have the same path living in Garden Grove and later attending Orange High. I often wish I would have asked the coaches about the former Olympian. I still have found no proof that the childhood classmate was really her sister as she had told me.

The years 1974–1976 would see more changes in music than ever before for me. Bands or groups like David Bowie, BTO, Gentle Giant, The Buzzcocks, Peter Frampton, Steve Miller, and many others would be the soundtrack in my mind to try and run faster.

So now it is 1975, and I am twelve years old, and I remember two ways the neighborhood kids would walk or run to Lampson Elementary School. The first way was the shorter way for those living on Anzio Street. This path we would walk south to the end of the street. Some would climb the high chain-linked fence or perhaps fit in a portion of the cut fence, if they could fit. We passed by the Crystal Wells apartments, which were blue and white in color at the time. Down the alley for a left turn past the mobile homes and you're at Lampson. The other way may be down Green Tree or Dawn Streets. Then to the end of one of those streets and then turn right. If you looked across the street, you would see the city shopping center now known as The Block.

Getting to School and the Start of a Bad Habit

The city shopping center was a large outdoor mall. This was the longer of the two ways. However, on the way home, many chose to walk the long way back. The reason for this was a small house an older lady owned. In her small living room, she had shelves of candy that ran around the perimeter of the room. She seemed to have every candy and more of that era. She would sit in her living room rocking chair with a small table next to it. On top of this table set, a locking metal box for making change. She then sold these various candies to the kids as they walked home from Lampson Elementary. Some candies seemed overpriced, and some were sold for just pennies. Some days we may complain she is ripping us off and other times said, "Wow, what a deal!"

Maybe that just depended on how much change we actually had in our pockets. Some kids did not like her, and others loved her. I guess she had good and bad days like the rest of us. Most days I would just run past it, as I did not always have change on me. No matter how much change you had, you were sure to find candy to purchase.

I have fond memories of looking forward to walking past this lady's house after school. During this time, I would enter the parks and recreation located at Ponderosa Park in Anaheim, California. I usually walked, ran, or rode my skateboard there. It was located north down Haster Street. This is where I would enter the 100-yard dash and represent the park against other parks in the city. This was the time of pulling up our tube socks, which lasted for years through to the '80s. I ended up taking second place in the city and received a second-place ribbon for my efforts. Many kids in our neighborhood were allowed to play until the streetlamps came on or might suffer repercussions. So yes, many times my legs have served me well. These were the days of drinking out of garden hoses, slip and slides, the big wheel, and numerous other games from those days.

I also remember, when I was eleven years old, many adults smoked, and this would be the year of my first cigarette. My biological father and stepfather smoked cigarettes. My stepfather had a distinctive way of smoking, where he would rest his thumb on his cheek and with his index and middle finger, bring the cigarette to his lips and perhaps blow a smoke ring or two. My stepfather smoked Marlboro Gold box 100s. My dad was that of a mechanic holding it in his mouth as long as he could before the ashes would fall. I seem to remember at that time it was a red and white box of Marlboros. So the curious boy in me tried one of my stepfather's Marlboro 100s. My neighbor who lived a couple doors down had made up a game we called pitcher catcher. One of us would pitch, and the other was the catcher. The catcher was also the umpire, and most of the time we agreed on what was a strike or not. We played it like six or nine inning baseball. His parents smoked Tareytons and Virginia Slims, and he was somewhat okay with sneaking some cigarettes for me to smoke later. I got a little hooked for about a year or so. So I guess that could have affected my running. I was lucky it did not seem to have a hindrance on me at the time.

7

CHAPTER

Saturday Playdays

Fourth grade had opened up a new world for me. This was back when I was actually ten. I remember the kids were quite competitive with games like tetherball, four square, and my favorite game of ball wall. Ball wall had the longest wait at recess. Recess or lunch, depending on how much time you had, might be spent waiting in line so you might overtake the champion.

There was also a noontime softball league. This was organized by one of the history teachers named Mr. Spanei. This would be especially competitive for the fifth and sixth graders in 1975 and 1976. The teams were pretty evenly matched and usually consisted of at least a couple or few better players on each team for the most part. This was similar to what we may see in major league baseball, just a comparison, of course. There were very good teams playing, and I felt in power as many would back up when I got up to bat. I remember this also was the case for a girl and boy also on one of my teams. Unfortunately, this did not translate for me as well to hardball when I played at the Northeast Garden Grove Little League in 1976. We also played kickball with one of two-sized red rubber balls, such as the ones used in four squares. There was also a competition in basketball to see who could make the most baskets out of twenty-five shots for a chance to represent various schools against other elementary schools. Now it is fourth grade, and it would be the first time starting a competition in sports versus other elementary schools, namely Handy, Taft, Serrano, Prospect, Cambridge, as well as numerous others. We had many sports, such as basketball, soccer, flag football, and Track. These sports were all played on Saturdays known as playdays, playday Saturdays or perhaps Saturday playdays, depending on who you talk to. The two sports that stand out for me most were flag football and track. We had these competitions from grades 4 through 6. Our practices were called "after-school sports," and our competitions, "playdays," were usually held every other Saturday throughout the year.

8

CHAPTER

Today is July 6, 2020. It is some forty-six years later, and I just got off the phone with one of the players of Handy, one of our rival schools, Handy a.k.a. the Hornets. His mom and my mom had worked at Kawasaki together. We talked for over an hour, and he gave me some great information as to some of their key players on the Handy Hornet team. We were the Lampson Leopards. My rival Hornet friend and I reminisced about those days, and he had said it was like free babysitting for our parents. He would suggest I call his friend and quarterback of the Handy Hornet team. It was nice to reminisce on these great childhood memories. This seems to be my only relocation of the fierce competition as other schools either crushed us or in a few cases, we won them. Sometimes the flags were one on each side, or there was another type that was one piece and is known today as a "triple-threat flag" that was used. I remember they were red, white, and blue at that time. For our team, I remember I was the quarterback for the Lampson Leopards. My step-cousin played halfback or tailback, depending on the play.

Today is July 6, 2020, and I just got off the phone. I decided to reach out to our city on Facebook. I started getting responses from males and females who remembered all the sports played in after-school sports, which led to the playday Saturdays. These included volleyball, basketball, soccer, flag football, and track and field, as well as the school and years played. This did spark many happy memories of our childhood and was the beginning of future sports in junior high together again.

July 6, 2020, and I just got a call from a friend of the Handy Hornet team. Our moms had worked together at Kawasaki. We have had minimal contact on Facebook and have not seen each other since our twentieth high school reunion. I found it to be so great, reminiscing of the days of our youth, and he gave me insight on the past Handy Hornets Elementary School flag football team. He then suggested I talk to the quarterback, who I did not remember crossing paths with since grammar school days. I texted him the next day a fairly long text. He texts me back, and we decide it would be better to converse by phone. He stated he would call me the next day, July 8. When he did not give me a call, I assumed he had forgotten and was busy, and I started writing again. I had just finished what I felt satisfied with what I wrote. Then I got a call, and it was the quarterback. My sugar was getting low, but I did not want to miss his call. I got a Coke, and we began talking. He too was a wealth of information of what had happened in the past. We went off topic so easily. I mean, it was so easy to remember the stars from other teams and friends we shared in common. I hope he felt as I did in enjoying the several-minute conversation we had. I hope to perhaps see each other when and if this Covid-19 pandemic ends.

So let's go back to 1975. The Lampson Leopards flag football team would carpool to other schools for competition. Sometimes we may take a bus. If we carpooled, everyone wanted to travel with one of the coaches who had a Black 66 Sporty Ford Mustang, which came with an eight-track player. In his car, he would play rock songs. Two songs I remember most hearing were "Crocodile Rock" and "Daniel" by Elton John, both of which had been out since 1972.

A fast car and loud music were definitely enough to get us pumped up. We had already played our rival school Handy for two years. We had formed a friendship with the Hornets, which seemed like two boxers may feel after a battle. We respected a well-played game. One game in particular would go back and forth, scoring touchdowns or being plagued with penalties and lose points we had already scored. For our team, I may pass for a score, but usually, either myself or my cousin might use a reverse for a score. I remember my cousin was quick and had a knack of running and spinning a full 360 degrees while maintaining forward momentum. He ran for about 10 yards and scored touchdowns. Perhaps I may even run with the ball to score.

The Handy team, more often than not, would use their very tall wide receiver to pass too by faking first to their halfback or even giving the ball to the halfback for the score. The game I seem to remember the most, in particular, is the Lampson Leopards and Handy. It looked like Lampson would win. It was the classic story of a team who was 7 points ahead in a high-scoring game and in this case, the Handy Hornets coming from behind and scoring two touchdowns, with very little time left. I think it was a runback touchdown after we had scored that tied us. Then Lampson would fumble, and the Hornets recovered the ball. The Hornets quarterback, who was very quick, decided to run a fake double reverse and then pass from the left side of the field to the right side of the field to the wide receiver to score and win by two touchdowns. No matter who we played, I only remember underhand congratulations to teams that won us or our team high-fiving one another if we won.

9

Elementary School Track Grades 4, 5, and 6

The next three years were the real start in track and field for me.

I have vague memories of fourth- and fifth-grade track. I know we were one of the very competitive teams. Lampson Elementary School was and still is the farthest school listed under the Orange Unified School District but located in Garden Grove, California. It was so close to the then city shopping center in Orange. I used to think it was in Orange, and if you crossed the street, you were in Garden Grove. However, this was not the case. There were and are elementary schools in Anaheim Hills that are also listed under the Orange Unified School District because of their proximity to district lines. We did not see most schools until the all-city track meets. The Anaheim Unified School District has always been separated by a set of railroad tracks. Canyon High School in Anaheim Hills, along with all the elementary and junior high schools under the Orange Unified District, was south, while north of the tracks is Esperanza High School in Anaheim under the Anaheim School District, and the same goes with their various schools north of the tracks. I am still amazed at how many schools were and are in the Orange District. In elementary school, it seemed so far away. The Leopards were such a short walk from the Garden Grove's school district. It was easy to see why the Orange District was so big to us. I know our team was good but by no means the best in the league. I am very lucky to still have two first-place medals. They are from the elementary school in the all-city meets. These meets would be held continuously at a hilltop junior high called Cerro Villa in Villa Park, California. Serrano Elementary, Cerro Villa, and Villa Park High School are within a rock-throw distance from one another and on the same street. And I have a picture to confirm one of the medals since they are tiny and have no event listed on them. I remember what I received in the sixth grade. The other I assume from just one year prior. Over the years, I have lost memorabilia, awards, or are broken. Perhaps more are in storage. I am fortunate to have kept a great deal of awards. Thanks to my mother who kept such good records of many of my years running. I only seem to remember the Orange Unified School District city-meets. As a Lampson Leopard, I would run sprints, such as the 100-yard dash and 440-yard relay. I would also participate in field events such as the long jump and even throw an 8-pound shot put.

The schools at that time that had the best athletes were from the Villa Park or Anaheim Hills area and included schools namely Serrano, Taft, Fletcher, Cambridge, Olive, Esplanade, and Walnut. The other schools we feared in Orange were Prospect and St John's Lutheran. The schools we were competitive with were La Veta; Sycamore, California; Glassell; and Handy. There were many more, such as Crescent, Villa Park, West Orange, and Fairhaven. I believe there was a Serra and perhaps many more, but the latter are the ones I remember. When it came to the Orange District meets, we would compete in heats until the schools were narrowed down to just nine for the finals. All the schools may have a year with a breakout star on their respective teams for their individual races or field events. This was usually the case in the Orange County all-city championships. In my sixth-grade year, my best and fondest memory was in the 1976 championships. It was in the 100-yard dash. I remember knowing a few of the kids from flag football and track from both years prior. However, many of the schools I had never even seen before. Looking back, I think we were at a quite disadvantage being at such a distance from the schools in the district.

The Start of Competition

We could have been easily in either the Garden Grove Unified or even the Anaheim Unified School Districts. In 1976, like always, it would be held on a Saturday. So many schools of many unknown talents to be up against. All the various schools I have spoken of seemed mysterious, and our hearts were pounding with excitement. I guess it may be feasible to say the same about the few members of our track squad. It was not until many of us saw him. He was a super tall guy, and many thought he had to be in ninth grade at least. To top it off, he had no school uniform. He was probably six feet two inches with blue jean shorts and just a plain white T-shirt with no known school affiliation. This would only add to mystique and other runners' skepticism. I know we must have asked. However, most of us thought he was just some type of "ringer." The nine of us all lined up in our blocks to start this race, and I feel confident they were as scared as me to run against this physically superior athlete. The gun goes off, and he and I and this six-foot-something runner were out ahead of the other runners as seen in a picture I have. The third-place runner was from Taft, and we would compete in future years. The tall guy I was racing had such a long stride. It seemed I had to run at least three strides for every one of his. I would say we had to be almost 10 yards ahead of the pack, with the third- and fourth-place runners barely visible in a black-and-white photograph my stepfather had taken. It is hard to decipher my win by the photograph. I assure you I barely nicked him at the line. I never ran against him again and always wonder what took place in his future.

I also have some memory of our team making it to the final with our four-man 440-yard relay team. I cannot begin to tell you of how exciting it was to see all the many teams arriving at this event, the mystery of what each team may have to offer, with all the buses arriving with not much heads up as to who was the best. This would be a much larger event than the maybe eight or so schools we had faced in flag football. In this all-city event, everyone was invited, and in fourth, fifth, or sixth grade could be anybody's year to have an individual champion, relay champion, or be an overall team champion. This same year in the relays sparks my memory of the 4x100-yards. Olive, Esplanade, and Fletcher are in a close race for the top spot. We would take fifth, but we were never last in the relays ever. This would be the last race of the championship meet. I am sure everyone in every school listed has a story of their own. In these events or other events, such as the 50-yard dash, or field events, such as the long jump or shot put, etc., because of after-school sports and playday Saturdays, I have made friendships that last to this day, and I will cherish forever.

CHAPTER 11

Years 1977–1979, Music Styles Change

The late '70s continued to bring in more styles of music: new wave, punk, and hard rock types of music. Bands I remember while running were Aerosmith, April Wine, The Brothers Johnson, The Clash, Gentle Giant, Gerry Rafferty, Joe Jackson, Journey, The Police, Styx, Sex Pistols, Judas Priest, and Van Halen. In 1978, I was fifteen, and I began an obsession of buying many LPs a.k.a. records of the bands I have just listed. I started listening to a boom box while practicing running on the track . Sometimes I would also listen to a boom box at various track meets if allowed. Some of the bands I listened to for one of their hits for pumping me up to run, such as in the case of Aerosmith's 1974 hit, "Train Kept a Rollin'."

The year was 1977, and the Lampson Leopards would need to take a bus to our new school known as the Portola Matadors a.k.a. Portoilet, as called by neighboring junior high schools. The Orange School District was unique at the time as our junior high was three years, and it included our freshman year of high school. Legend would have it we should not wear a belt to school on the first day of school or risk being hung up by our belt on a chain-linked fence. The day came, and maybe a few were threatened, but nothing happened. So much was happening though. We were riding skateboards, beach cruisers, having many forms of music to listen to, and it is debatable on whether music was in its prime in these years. I remember my cousin, another friend, and I would do handstands on our skateboards. My cousin was the one I had given credit to for using a bicycle tube to jump over stacked skateboards. I would use it to jump over curbs. However, I just found a YouTube video from 1975 that told of kids doing these very things on skateboards, which we started doing maybe a year later and was filmed in Huntington Beach, California.

I started needing to eat more snacks as insulin reactions came more frequently. I remember one time, in particular, a guy coming up to me and telling me to give him my chips, and I said I was weak and I needed them. He would chase me until the bell rang, and luckily, I did not go unconscious this time.

Portola was down the street from, in my opinion, two very iconic local restaurants, The Chili Pepper and Original Sam's Pizza. I have been going to The Chili Pepper since I was ten. They served delicious Mexican food. It was inexpensive yet seemed nice enough to take a date too. The Original Sam's Pizza, I believe, had the best pizza I ever had. It was located across the street from the St. Joseph's Hospital in Orange, California. It was in what we called a "hole in the wall" in a strip mall. I never witnessed anyone who could eat a whole large thick-crust pizza by themselves. We always seemed to have leftovers of this great pizza. Unfortunately, neither restaurant is with us any longer. The Chili Pepper had been open for some fifty years.

In my seventh- and eighth-grade years of track, I would be reintroduced to a new set of friends who I remembered only slightly from elementary school competition from track and flag football. Elementary school kids from schools like Sycamore, West Orange, and perhaps others west of Main Street in the city of Orange would all become "Portola Matadors." Elementary schools east of main and closer to my future high school would go to Yorba Junior High a.k.a, "Your-butt" as a rebuttal to our junior high being called "Portoilet."

Junior high track would see new stars from schools like Cerro Villa, Vista Del Río, El Rancho, Santiago, and McPherson. Additionally, there was Yorba, Peralta, and my school, Portola. Cerro Villa, El Rancho, and Vista Del Río were in the north. I still wonder what the school kids in the north must've eaten as they were bigger and better. The Cerro Villa track star would choose baseball as his future love, but he was the fastest in the league. If he had time, he would enter some of the varsity team events, such as sprints and relays. Cerro Villa would have the best team in all the junior high teams.

Depending on the year, race or field event, there would be years of different stars and those who may change sports or move that are not accounted for. I have limited Super 8 films or awards I have received. This, of course, is in no way me trying to state I was any better than other athletes. However, I have chosen to focus on just two events, the 100-yard dashes and two 440-yard relays, which are based off the Super 8 mm film given to me, from my mother, some years ago. What I figure was the prelims for the league championship were at Portola Junior High.

The Portola Matadors would also win the 400-yard relay in the prelims, which I anchored.

The first race was the 100-yard dash. I had played tackle football, and the Cerro Villa star could not be caught and scored often. On film, you could tell there were some stars who had not been in the meet prior. This would show by seeing the footage that this was the league championships which was held at Fred Kelly Stadium in Orange, California. At this meet, the same schools would be there with bigger kids and this time the star from Cerro Villa. I will briefly say I remember this star also played with the giant members of the Cerro Villa Junior High tackle football team. I never tackled this star, and their team would easily tromp us. Conservatively, I will say, I think, the score of that game was 44-0.

There would be a couple more stars from the Santiago squad as well as the McPherson team. My first race was my favorite as this race would be prior to the final 440 relay race that would follow last. This race was the 100-yard dash. There would be nine men who now lined up in the blocks and, I believe, were the best of the best sent for their respective schools.

The gun went off, and myself and the star of Cerro Villa were quickly out first. I see I am only slightly ahead of the Cerro Villa star, and I would jot back and forth for first position, but it was definitely a photo finish. The Cerro Villa star would dive over the line. I thought they gave it to me as they said my leg was ahead first. However, the rules state the chest is the body part that is supposed to be judged as crossing the rope first. I have a still-shot photo of us at the line and trying to see who crosses with the chest first. His head is ahead and my leg. If I am honest, I believe he won this race. However, this is the closest I would ever get in a race with him and never raced him again. By the time we had finished this race, we were probably a good 10 yards ahead of the field. The fight for third was between Cambridge and Santiago. It looks like one of the two Santiago stars at the last second would edge out Cambridge for a third-place finish. The last race that ended the city of Orange championships was the 4x110-yard dash. The stars from Cerro Villa and Santiago would make me pay dearly in this next race. The next race we had a different member to start in the blocks on the first leg of the 4x110. The time of the first hand off we were second to last in the race. Our second leg would make up quite a bit of ground and be even with Santiago and Vista Del Río. Being probably five yards ahead at this point, it was Vista Del Río, and Cerro Villa almost even, and Portola was in third. Cerro Villa pulls ahead of Vista Del Río, and we are probably 10 yards behind Vista Del Río and Cerro Villa. However, we would win by a large margin. The city prelims were at Portola. The third leg gained the week prior first place before handing it to me. We would win by a large margin. The next week was the city finals. The Cerro Villa team was all new players, except for the one that anchored last week in the third position first.

My stepfather had taped the race on 8mm film. This is where I believe the race was won. The man in the third position for Cerro Villa was the same young man who anchored the prelims from a week before for Cerro Villa, and he handed the baton to the Cerro Villa star from the 100-yard dash race earlier. Out of nowhere, Santiago's third leg would now hand off to their very quick anchor in second position. I am in fourth place at the hand off with McPherson now slightly ahead of me for third position. At this point, the Super 8 film runs out. From my recollection, I was able to almost run down the runner from Santiago, but he would edge me out for second place, and Cerro Villa, as expected, would win this final. We had to settle for third place.

12

CHAPTER

High School Year 1980

The year was now 1980, and the various schools that competed in junior high would merge in high school. For example, our Portola Matadors and the Yorba Toros would merge to become the Orange High Panthers in Orange, California. This same year would dawn several groups or musical styles to choose from. Sometimes they may even cross into one another. Some were just extensions of the late '70s. You could be a rocker or metal head. You may be a punker who also liked to be goth. Maybe you were a mod who liked ska music. Perhaps a new-waver who liked alternative music. Or maybe you were a skater and a surfer, a sporto or stoner. We may belong to more than one of these groups of people. Many establishments would cater to these forms of groups. But for now, I will just say it was easy to get lost in the many genre of music in 1980. As far as music, rap would begin its journey to replace disco. Rock, hard rock, punk rock, ska, new wave, and goth would all gain momentum. Some of the music I would listen to in 1980 were Black Sabbath, Devo, The Clash, Genesis, Pink Floyd, Molly Hatchet, Missing Persons, and too many more to name. Most often I would still have someone hold up a boom box to a song by Aerosmith or Missing Persons when I ran a 220-yard dash, especially for the 440 race.

OHS and other high schools would be currently three-year instead of four-year high schools in the Orange School District. The first day at Orange High School, I was driving a green Vega hatchback. My stepfather had sold this car to me for a loan of $500 and $50 a month for payments. I would make the trip from my home in Garden Grove, exactly 7.8 miles away, to Orange High.

The first day of school, I was a little over a block away from the school, and my car stopped and was smoking. Driving behind me unknown to me was a teacher who stopped to help me. The car was smoking, and I noticed the oil light had come on. The car had blown up. This was my fault as I had not changed the oil. This same teacher I would have a class with on that same day. Of course, it was an embarrassing moment for me.

I was continuing to smoke cigarettes on the weekends with some drinking, which escalated through my high school years. I felt uncomfortable at this school and do not remember really having friends I had grown up with in my classes. I still excelled at sports and found this to be my favorite time at OHS. My favorite classes besides track were history and PE, especially during track season. I would soon find that most of my best friends were mostly juniors and seniors on the track team with some exceptions from my Lampson Elementary and/or Portola Junior High School days.

Just prior to joining the track team, one of the juniors had given me the nickname "Lighting" to describe how fast he thought I was.

One of my best friends as a senior would call me, "Hey, Sophomore." Someone had given him the name like Farrah Fawcett to describe his feathered hair. He was a good-looking dude, and we became not only good friends, but he was also quite the sprinter.

Another senior who partied with us on weekends was nicknamed "Chicken," as a term for his skinny legs and how fast he could run. I guess it's like a chicken. We smoked cigarettes, drank alcohol, and sometimes smoked marijuana at one time or another. Chicken had a blue Ford Pinto he used to like to drive.

Chicken, Farrah, and I would sometimes drive around the street corners, and Chicken would pull on the emergency brake to fishtail around various corners. This scared me but also made me laugh. A lot of people did similar things like this. These were the days when seat belts were not required. That law would not go into effect until 1984. Luckily, we did not get hurt, same as other friends I knew at this time. However, this was just getting lucky, as plenty would not fare quite as well in the future.

On the track, we still would win plenty of relay races together, races such as the 440-yard relay, the mile relay, and fifth of all time in the sprint medley for our school Orange High. The races were also run with various more dedicated runners. The star triple-jumper and the star 880 runner would alternate as a fourth member with us to contribute to some of our winnings. We were having fun and ran because we could.

Farrah had given us the name "Domo Brothers." He would say because we "dominate" the races. This would stick with me, and I would mention them later in my high school yearbook as "Domo Brothers," one with their initials.

I had been working at the UA City Cinemas since the summer of 1979 as a way to earn money for the things I wanted to do at the time, things like paying car payments, gas, food, buying records, and dating girls periodically. Working at the UA is a book unto itself with the friendships I made and the many adventures we shared together. There too I would work with guys a couple of years older who mostly went to either Orange High or Santa Ana High School, also in Orange County. My best friends from there are still mostly available to this day.

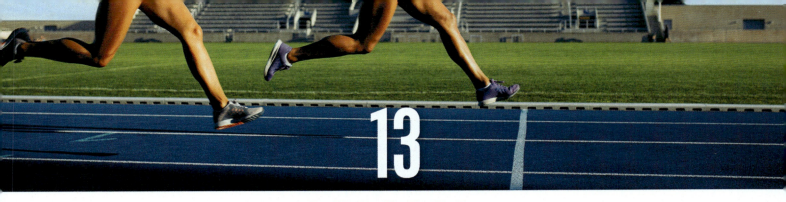

13

CHAPTER

The 1980 Track Team and Our Legendary Coach

I think the reason I had always ran track is it gave me a sense of accomplishment and purpose.

To get told I was the fastest on the team in the sprints and being on the varsity squad felt good to a damaged, depressed ego. Before track season had started, I was out looking at the track after school. I noticed a guy sitting on a bicycle who was staring at me as if he wanted to beat me up. I was afraid, but there were two kids next to him who said hi to me and apparently watched me run before and said that I was so fast. Then the gentleman on the bicycle says I can beat him in a race, though I had not raced the 440-yard track before, yet I still had sprinted that far or farther in my neighborhood. I said, "I bet you I can smoke a cigarette and race you around this track and win."

The two kids said, "I bet he can," and that they would not take that bet.

He then says, "No, that's okay."

I felt empowered, but quite honestly, I was relieved and really am not sure if I would have won that proposed race.

The next week I would join the track team and meet the head coach and legend of the 440-yard dash. He was the state record holder as a junior with a time of 48.8. This race was held at the thirty-fourth annual track-and-field championships, which was on May 24, 1952. This was a Saturday at the Los Angeles Coliseum. He also won the southern section again a year later according to the CIF record books. These records are still held in the CIF records located in Los Alamitos, California, though the southern section record would be broken many times from such runners from Santa Ana and Riverside as well as others in the southern section. The Orange Unified record was still yet to be broken. It was now twenty-eight years later, and the record still stood. This day I would also meet the assistant coach as well as the cross-country-distance coach. The head coach would have sayings like "To be a winner, 'I' must be a winner all of the time because winning is a habit . . .," "No stinkin' thinkin'," or "Garbage in, garbage out." He had also taught our whole track squad "to be all you can be."

I would continue where I left off from Portola Junior High with the 100-yard dash and the 220-yard dash. Our track team would be told this year about talks of the races going to the metric system.

I do not believe we ever ran in meters. According to "Wiki," this was, indeed, the year of that very change. At the time, we were told that meters would be 10 yards further. Some sites will claim 100 yards is farther than 100 meters. We know, of course, this is not the case by the times of the compared races. I assume the correct distance is 109.631 yards further for the 100 meters versus the 100-yard dash to be the correct conversion. I am sure it is a debatable subject. Probably my favorite race for the 100-yard dash was my race at the Laguna Beach Trophy Meet. This was different from the Orange County track-and-field championships and was located at Laguna Beach High School until 1983. The championships were based with over sixty Orange County schools. I would take third place in the 100-yard dash.

Laguna Beach seemed to be different, and it was the only time I ran as a sophomore because of the caliber of runners. It felt like there may be LA schools at this meet, but I cannot confirm that in any way this was true. LA schools were known to have faster times. However, thinking back, this was all of Orange County. This would include other leagues.

Someone would do well later in the state CIF championships in this very race from Santa Ana Valley was in our league. I do not even remember there being a heat to qualify for this nine-man race. In my photograph, it shows lane 3, lane 5, and lane 6 with the best starts. I was in lane 7. The gentleman in lane 6 would have a battle with me for the second-place finish as lane 5 would win. Lane 6 and I would actually have a very close race for second place, in which he would prevail and had given me the third-place medal block award. Though I had a pretty good start, a photo taken shows my form was not in full stride like lanes 6, 5, and 3 were. The man to my right, in lane 6, and lanes 3 and 5 had the best starts and form, and because of this, I would still be happy with the third-place medal block I had received. However, I would fare better in the 220-yard dash with a second-place finish, also in the sophomore division of this same meet.

To be honest, I have no recollection of the 220-yard race. For some reason, I only know I was finding better success at the longer sprint races now. I have made several attempts to find a program or a list of schools at this meet. I have not been able to confirm this and only have my medal and photo as proof of the 100-yard dash race. I only ran in this event one time. The first- and second-place finishers would qualify to go on to the Arcadia Invitational located in the San Gabriel Valley of LA County. This would seem to be the peak of my 100-yard-dash days.

The year 1979 had been a great year for the OHS track team, with times not being broken in 1980, such as the case in the mile relay. However, in 1980, records from the year before would be broken by the same boys as in the case of this particular star who broke his record in 1979 of 6 feet 3 inches to 6 feet 5 inches in the high jump.

Another tall star would soon focus on breaking the triple-jump all-league record in the future. Some of us would set new records either as a sophomore in a varsity competition and/or overall. I was fortunate to be one of the ones who had a record in my grade and overall. Such as was the case in the 220 curve with a 22.4. This was just for my school records. I also had a sophomore record for the 100-yard dash of 10.2.

Our head coach had talked about me adding the 440-yard dash to my list of races. I wanted no part of this at the time as I thought it was way too far. One day the assistant coach was holding a stopwatch as I practiced the 220-yard race. He blew his whistle, and I was off. He clicks his stopwatch and yells across the field to the head coach and yells a time I cannot remember now. He walks over to the head coach who smirks and says, "Run it again," and I would soon be a 440-yard dash runner in the relay races as well.

A day or two later, I was in recess, and my sugar was very low, according to my blood test I had just taken. I got in the snack line and bought a package of chocolate doughnuts and a chocolate milk. I had eaten about four of the mini doughnuts and about half of the chocolate milk. The head coach came over to me and said, "Why are you eating this? It is not good for you," and slaps me slightly.

He then threw the rest of my snacks away. I screamed, "My sugar was low!"

The bell had just rung, and we went our separate ways. I remembered this was when I felt like he was my stepfather. However, my stepfather would say things like "Don't let the door hit you on the ass when you go out," if I wanted to go somewhere, as a form of my approval to leave.

Later I would find out their birthdays were on March 5. Later I would understand that I was cared for more than I had thought at the time. Little did the Orange High coach know I also smoked cigarettes, smoked pot, and drank alcohol on the weekends.

The year 1980 would introduce me to our relay team. We ran in an invitational that introduced me to a very fast man from Edison High School in Huntington Beach, California. He was out of our league figuratively and literally. This gentleman would set all-time records that still hold true to this day in the list of all-time records, such as the 40-yard, 60-yard, and 100-yard dashes, the latter race being the most notable. He was also well known for being a star running back in football as he was on his high school championship football team in 1979.

In 1980, one of the highlights for me was when I ran a leg of the 440 relays against him, in which he "smoked me." The latter was said in those days as someone who was excitedly fast, but we still took fifth place, which was respectable for a race of that caliber and in this particular invitational.

Invitationals are events that are entered usually based on the schools that had the best times and based on the available entries. Some relay invitationals had unlimited entries. I wish I could tell you which one this was called. Since we did not win a medal, I cannot find documentation on this, YouTube was not available yet, and I had not been aware of the actual CIF records that would have been available to us.

In 1980, Orange High School was in the Century League. The most feared man to run against in the Century League sprint races was a gentleman from Santa Ana Valley High School also known as Valley High School. Valley was a four-year high school, and the year prior, he set a Century League record of 23 feet 1 inch in the long jump as a freshman. He would be known to be the fastest in the 100-yard dash as well as the 220-yard. He only improved as time went on.

I have a vivid memory of a 220 race I had against him at Orange High School (OHS). This was probably the race where I obtained my high school record. The star from Valley usually won his races in the 220 by as many as 10 yards and had a habit of waving to people and assuming he would always win, which was usually the case. The Valley runner was in lane 5, and I was in lane 2. The gun goes off, and the Valley star is out like a rocket, entering the turn of the race, and he has a commanding lead, and as soon as he enters the straightaway, he begins his customary waving. This had angered me, and little did he know, I came off the turn almost even with him as he started waving. I was able to take him at the finish. I cannot tell you of the joy I and my teammates felt and the joy of seeing him looking astonished that he had lost a race. Since this 220-yard dash was probably not a "sanctioned" race, it would not be listed in more record books, which would have held more prestige. However, the fact still remains that I won SAV's ace in our track meet with Santa Ana Valley.

Toward the end of 1980, I would get a green Toyota mini truck. I had always admired a friend's red Datsun mini truck.

14

CHAPTER

Cars

Some cars I had a green Vega I had been driving from my stepfather had been at my fathers in Buena Park, California. He had promised to try and fix it. However, he had not been able to work on it, and I was in need of a vehicle. My mother had not been interested in the hot rod I wanted to purchase. She and my stepfather agreed to look at vehicles as they were not pleased with my father's lesser-safe primer-colored Gremlin vehicle he had given to me. The Gremlin was a part-gray primer-colored car, and the driver's side door was held on by only a rope. I saw the green mini truck and hoped I could fix it up similar to my friend's or other ones I saw in mini truck clubs in those days. My mother and stepfather agreed to loan me the down payment as long as I promised to make the car payments. It is debatable on the payments of this car. As I had stated before, I was currently working at a movie theater. On the weekends, many of us worked a shift from 6:00 p.m. to 2:00 a.m., with an hour break before the midnight movies would start. I was only sixteen at this time. The UA theater at the city shopping center would show four movies, which ran in a straight line with four doors across. At any given time, there would be one cashier, two or three behind the snack bar, and one to three watching people who tried to sneak into the wrong theater.

This Saturday my friend and I were the ones to go on a "beer run" during our hour break before the midnight movies would start. I drove, and one of my senior friends was able to buy beer in Garden Grove at a liquor store close to "Me And Eds" pizza parlor.

On this night, we were running a little late returning to our shift and having enough time to consume some of the beer we had purchased. I came into the parking lot a little quickly, and a guy said, "You almost hit me!"

He then produced a chain and started toward me. My fellow worker gets out of the vehicle. I find out he knows the guy from his high school. The guy says hi and tells him how lucky it was that my fellow worker was with me and that he would have beat my ass. My work friend says to him that I had just beaten the Santa Ana Valley star sprinter in the 220-yard dash. He then says, "You 'smoked' him, wow!"

He then fist-bumps me. I tried to downplay it because I thought it was just luck. I proceeded to explain what had transpired. I was so relieved and felt I had actually made a friend. I then apologized to him if I had come close to hitting him.

He said, "No problem, man."

As far as another favorite highlight for me, it is almost the end of track season at OHS. I remember again that this was when I would run relays as a 440-yard runner. We would take a second-place finish at the Santa Ana relays in the mile relay. We also took first place in the sprint medley at the Rotary Relays. I have decided to reference some of my closest friends with the nicknames we gave one another.

It is currently late July 2020, and I just ran across an article about our 1980 OHS head coach, and I began to cry. I did not know of some of the difficulties he had growing up. I still have messages from 2010 that said he had quit the coaching track after fifty-one years. He e-mailed me, saying he had to hang it up because of health issues.

Little did I know, just two years prior, a Canyon High School junior had broken his fifty-six-year-old Orange District record. It was a southern sanctioned state record. In 2008, a junior from Canyon High School ran a 48.4 with Coach's adjusted 440-yard time to meters, which was 48.5. Coach also had a time of 48.94 on a curve track.

I wished I had discussed with him the demons I have faced. In 2010, I had rambled on to him in my texts as I was at the time taking antidepressants. In recent years, I would find that this really was not the correct remedy for my problems. I would text him off and on until 2014. I know he must have known I was having health issues by the responses to my texts. I have recently read my texts from my OHS coach, and my last text received from him was dated June 7, 2014. I wrote a couple more times and wished him a happy birthday in March 2015. By this time, he was in and out of the hospital and would pass away on October 4, 2017, at the age of eighty-two.

Myself and a fellow track team member, as well as many others of different years who were coached by him, attended the service. I wish I would've known more about him in 1980, for I as well as some others may have taken this sport more seriously and might have been able to achieve even more together in our events and as a track team. I still miss him for the man he was and the man he became. I was blessed to be a sophomore running on the varsity team and setting a record time of 22.4 in the 220-yard dash and a 100-yard dash time of 10.2.

I would take first place in the 100-yard dash at the Century League Jamboree. I was also blessed to be a part of several different relays, such as a first place sprint medley relay team at the Rotary Relays, as well as many second-place finishes in such events as our varsity mile-relay team and in many different events. So in just one year at Orange High School, I was a part of a quite successful track team and so happy to share so many memories and happy moments together.

One of the relay members would set an Orange District record in the triple jump of 45 feet 7 ¾ inches for the year 1980. Additionally, the four-mile-relay team set the school record with a time of 18.01. Our track squad would take second place overall in the large schools division of the Eddie West's relays held at Santa Ana College. All this and more for the Orange High Panthers of 1980.

15

CHAPTER

The Decision to Switch High Schools 1981

In about August 1980, my parents had made the decision to move to a house they found on Euclid Street close to El Modena High School in Orange, California. Ironically, my girlfriend at the time lived just fourteen houses down from our soon-to-be new home.

It is now 1981. Some of the bands I listened to before racing were namely AC/DC, Def Leppard, Foreigner, Missing Persons, Rush, Suburban Lawns, Scorpions, The Vandals, and still Van Halen, anything that came out and pumped me up before I ran.

Many of the ElMo Kids could be seen spending their lunch hour at the local Naugles restaurant. Most of these would later become Del Taco today. It was just down the street from our school. It had tasty Mexican food with large portions. Many of us also frequented Naugles for lunch. I could also be seen working on weekends at a local movie theater. It was originally called The Village Theater before changing names to "The Villa" a.k.a. "Villa Park Twin Cinema." I worked there for extra money. It was very small. You walk down a small set of stairs to reach the ticket window on the left. When you enter the theater, the middle showcased the snack bar. The movies would have just one theater on each side of the snack bar counter placed directly in the center. It was located in Orange but was named after a small suburb nearby, which is still only about two miles long known as Villa Park.

I still frequented the Record Trading Center (RTC) to purchase used vinyl records. The Orange County punk band Lost Cause would form and actually record their *Lost Corners* record in the following year. This would happen at the transformed studio in back of the RTC.

The year 1981 would be the final year of the local favorite skatepark, The Big O, after having a three-year run.

16
CHAPTER

The Parties and Orange County Punk

Orange County punk band Lost Cause would play at the legendary Cuckoo's Nest and would have various lineup changes of their guitarist and bassist. I found punk music at this time to be mysterious, scary, and intriguing. I had only listened to punk music from the UK before hearing the bands coming from Orange County. This, for me, was the beginning of "kegger parties," in which you may see Orange County punk or rock bands. The parties would have kegs of beer and a cover charge at the door or gate by the side of the house. Usually, the most intimidating guy could be found to watch and take money upon entering. This, many times, was to assure more kegs could usually be purchased throughout the evening if the party had not been broken up by the local authorities.

One guy I knew who had no fear once drove me through the parking lot of the Cuckoo's Nest. This was during the time of fighting between the punks and the cowboys from the Cowboy bar next door. Stories of fights had surfaced. The Vandals punk band even had a song out about it titled "Urban Struggle."

Lost Cause had their album *Born Dead* and released a 7-inch EP out. I knew some of the members of Lost Cause from going to junior high with some of the future members. I only knew of the scene through mostly rumors that would turn out later to be true. I would continue to buy vinyl LPs from my favorite new and used record store, Record Trading Center (RTC). I had been buying from them since junior high.

This year I had the opportunity to stay at OHS or transfer to El Modena High School. This was within walking distance of our soon-to-be new home. I did not want to drive past El Modena every day and have to leave probably thirty minutes earlier to try and reach OHS on time for school. I also felt I would have a better shot at winning a track championship with the Vanguard team.

It is 1981, and my best friend at the time was also transferring from Orange High to El Modena High a.k.a. ElMo. We would share in our adventures of partying. He convinced me to skip school for the first two days and told me we have until we check in to school to worry about the absences. He also introduced me to a perm-haired guy who used to wear handkerchiefs around his neck, and we had copied his attire idea.

As I would play my boom box, blaring an early hit of Def Leppard "Rock Brigade," he would whistle with a loud YA! He did this in between going to our next classes. We all three had started school on the third day before attending El Modena High School.

Later I would try to attempt his whistle and "ya" yell with great failure. We did this, I think, as a way of communicating where we were in between classes. As we had skipped the first couple of days of school, we had done so to watch a local band rehearsing in a storage-type unit located next to the garage. It had a little room to watch them rehearse while drinking beers, such as Lucky's Lager, Lowenbrau, or whatever was available to us in those days. The band was called Vesuvius. We would additionally listen to records from the likes of The Scorpions' seventh album titled *The Zoo*. Ufo and whatever else rocked at the time. This would continue on and off most weekends, and a good percentage of us would do this while having a pretty frequent smoking habit. Some of us tried to master a trick of laying a cigarette on the underside of our wrist and flipping it straight into our mouths.

17

CHAPTER

My New High School

On my first day of school, my third-period class was history. It was unknown to me at the time that this was the cross-country coach. He would have a lot of influence on our track team's future events and the track team would enter into.

During this class, I was visited by the head football coach. He coached a very successful ElMo football team. He asked the history coach to see me. The history teacher seemed displeased as he was a teacher who took his classes seriously. The football coach then welcomed me to the school and complimented me on my past track experiences. He then asked me if I thought about going out for football and said he could see me as a running back with my speed. Since it was at the same time as track, I said I did not want to take a chance of getting hurt. I also wanted to dedicate myself to track. He smiled and said, "Well, think about it." This same man would be the coach of three southern section football championships before retiring in 1985.

The head track coach seemed to grin when I showed up to practice. I would learn he was also the assistant head football coach. He said, "I heard the coach asked you to join the football team."

I would then see some of the football players who were also on the track team, such as the quarterback and the football team's star running back. They would run when they did not have a football game. This star running back would do well in the sprints and the hurdles. I would also see the Century League and record holder of the 100-yard dash, who had run it in 10.3, at the 1980 Orange County championships.

Many of the track squad had already known I was coming to El Modena. We had known one another from previous years of running against one another. In fact, the best-known sprinter at ElMo would exchange an ElMo sweatshirt for my Orange High jacket at one of the track meets, when I ran at OHS. We respected our speed, and we had become good friends.

A sprint coach was added to our team later this year. He was similar to the head coach at OHS. The difference was he actually would get in the blocks and demonstrate how to explode out of the blocks. He had great form. We had speculated on the coach's age as we were amazed how fast he was. Someone had asked how old he was, and he would say he is almost seventy. He was actually fifty-two. We would see him more frequently in the following year.

My history teacher was also the cross-country-distance coach. He would take a big part in handling our future as a team. He also would take a key role in getting us entered into more advanced meets in the Los Angeles area.

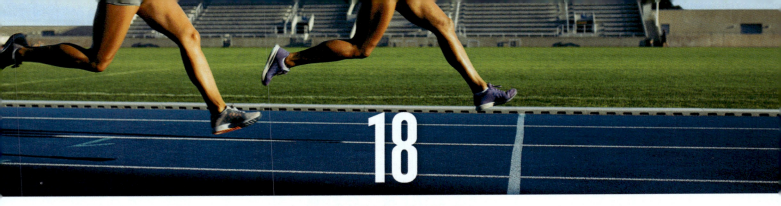

18

CHAPTER

Our Top Runners

I have decided to focus on six sprinters and one cross-country-distance runner. Three were sophomores, three were juniors, and one distance runner star, who was a senior. The first sprinter-distance runner was a sophomore and was already a star 880 runner for El Modena. The following two years, he would break school records and Orange County records. These would be in the 880 as well as being on three notable record-breaking relay teams. The latter was just on the track team. He also would break several cross-country records. His cross-country accomplishments were multiple and may not all be mentioned. I also should mention he would become a state champion in the 1600 just a couple of years later. So he had the distinction of being on the track and cross-country teams. I like to call him the "dedicated runner." You could always see him running far distances throughout our neighborhood. When I spoke to this runner on the phone, he said he had also held records in some sprint races at McPherson Junior High. These records were in sprint races, such as the 100-yard and 220-yard races. His future, however, would be in the 880, mile, two-mile, and mile relay. I always thought this dedicated runner would go to the Olympics.

The second sophomore was a tall sprinter who was very well gifted in the field events. This *humble track star* would be best known for a relay race and fantastic field event school record the following year. He always seemed calm with a quiet demeanor.

The third runner was a sophomore whose last name means a horse running fairly fast with bouncing steps. He would be a member of a future school record on the mile-relay team. He also ran the hurdles in 1982.

The fourth was a junior who was also known for being great in the hurdles and sprints. He was also the star running back for the El Modena Vanguard football team. He was a sure bet to place in everything he ran in when he was available for the track squad. He would later be known as "The Blur." This would become his nickname in 1982.

The fifth man was what I liked to call "the "Comedian." He was also known as Nueby. He was the kind of guy you might say, "I dare you too," and of course, he would. He was also the Century League champ in the 100 in 1980. Additionally, he ran the 220 and on our 440 and mile-relay teams.

As for myself, the sixth sprinter and a junior in 1981, I would be in the 100, 220, 440, 440-relay, and mile-relay teams. Since you could only have four events in a meet, it really depended on who did not have a football game to take the 100 and give us valuable points to win track meets.

Last was the senior distance runner, best known for the tenth best time nationwide of all time in the 3,200 meters in this year. He would be on the iconic distance medley later this year. That would also be my favorite and most exciting race to watch and be a part of in 1981. The latter I will discuss later.

This year would have different seniors in the sprints. For example, the 440-yard-relay team. Sometimes El Mo's quarterback as well as other senior sprinters. I mention another junior briefly here as he was the one on Santiago's junior high school 440-yard-relay team, in which he anchored. He also would do very well in the field events. He was the Century League champion in 1980 for the long jump. He jumped 21 feet 7 inches. I always wondered why he stuck to just the field events in high school.

Coming from Orange High School, I had, indeed, missed some of my childhood friends. My decision to go to ElMo was a blessing and a curse as my relationships would be altered by the bad decisions I was about to make. This part of my story, I have struggled for weeks to write about. I could write a book alone on apologies to those I hurt this year, and so I am doing so here.

I never seemed to stick to just one thing. It was me never wanting to miss a thing and what I may do and bring me more pleasure. I think the real truth I ran was for the admiration I received and the camaraderie, the feeling like I belonged to a type of family with its solidarity, perhaps also of feeling liked and sometimes adored that did not hurt my ego.

The 1981 varsity track squad would prove to be quite stellar. Myself and my fellow sprinters would now be taking first place in events that otherwise I had usually taken second place with the OHS squad. Our team took first in the Century League championships in the 440-yard relay and in the mile relay, which would prove to be our best relay event bearing El Modena's iconic distance medley. We would have some success in all the latter relays. This also accounts for many future invitational entries, such as the Arcadia Invitational and the Mt. Sac Relays held in Walnut, California. The mile relay team would take third in the Orange County championships in the mile relay. This was out of twenty-four schools. There was a qualifier race and then the final. Additionally, we would finish first in three events at the Rotary Relays, the mile-relay as well as the 4x220 and the 4x110. I would take first in the Century League 440-yard dash and a second-place finish in the 220-yard dash. My guess is it was probably Santa Ana Valley's star sprinter who would beat me in the 220. He was not about to lose two times in a row. I am sure there were other events we entered and did respectable in, but these are the only events I have proof of. There was another race rarely run, except in certain relays or invitationals. This particular race would prove to be my favorite of all races in 1981. It was called the distance-medley relay. I will tell you later about this iconic race, but first, let me explain . . .

19

CHAPTER

Decisions I Made 1981

I have been told by some that I always wanted to be all things to all people, and I think this is still true. If a friend said, "Let's go somewhere," I wanted to go, especially if it was some type of party. A great deal of the time I could not live in the moment. This is something my mom said to me, and I agree she was correct at the time. I always felt I was missing something more, and I freely gave in to temptation. I had fought it by going to youth groups at the Garden Grove Community Church (GGCC). However, the excitement of parties, girls, and soon drugs would enter my life and keep me from perhaps another path. Still, this year, as far as track, I would win a great number of races, especially in the league. I am a type 1 diabetic who has already not gotten along well with his parents. In retrospect, many times it was my fault. They had very little knowledge of my use of drugs as a way to cope with what I felt at home. However, I do give credit to my parents for coming to a number of my sporting events. Additionally, they also came to several meets to show their support when they could.

20
CHAPTER

Crazy Times

I was also a smoker and drinking alcohol on the weekends. Then I would meet a guy a couple of years older who graduated from Saugus High School but now worked in Steel Fabrication down the street from my school. I helped him through a rough time in his life. He had been living at his uncle's shop, where he took showers with a hose. I gave him some canned goods from our house. This guy always made me laugh and knew where the best parties were. He always seemed positive and seemed to always have an uncanny way of getting away with things that others perhaps would not. He soon would get an apartment close to our high school and was known for having "ragers" or the "raddest" parties. I remember the last party he had. Guys wanted to use the only restroom in his apartment. He proceeded to kick holes in the walls and exposed the two-by-fours in the walls then urinated in a beer cup on the walls and said he would concrete over them when he moved out the next day. Another time, he said, "Hey, man, I need your help," and then said, "Hold this shit a second." Yes, he was holding a turd in his hand.

I was eating a steak and sprang up from the chair to push his hand back. He just laughed as I almost vomited.

He then sprayed shaving cream on my door of a giant penis. This permanently stained my bedroom door.

He kept me on my toes for sure.

It was probably 1983, when this nightclub called Circus Circus opened in Santa Ana, California. It was an eighteen-and-over club with a bar for those twenty-one and older. Another friend said he was able to alter the year on the license to appear as if we are twenty-one. So we, eighteen-year-olds, started going to the bar and getting into this nightclub and drinking.

Half the schools practically always drank beer and had parties on the weekends. In fact, one guy's dad from our school worked for Coors and would have parties too. My old friend and I were the envy of others as we would get into the Circus Circus with fake IDs. After others had the same idea to get into clubs, it quickly stopped. The secret was out. If the bouncers or police held the license up to a light, they could see the line where it had been cut, and they would be arrested or stopped from entering the establishment. So we enjoyed going, and I had another idea. I had some passes from one of the theaters I had worked for. I started bribing them to get into the nightclub instead of paying the cover charge. I figured I would not be allowed to drink. They started asking with their stamp in hand, "Over or under?"

I said over and pointed to my friend who had a mustache, and I said he is with me. Since I never got into any kind of trouble and the bouncers enjoyed the periodic gifts, I was forever allowed to drink in the nightclub while still in our teens.

I remember seeing the band Felony and Greg Khin there in 1983. They would close soon after for having the same club name as the hotel in Las Vegas. Cheap food and drinks, a lot of fun times we had in those days.

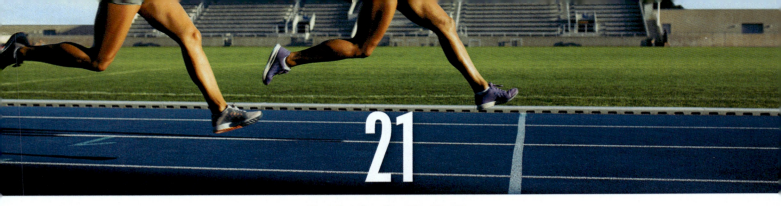

21
CHAPTER

The Distance-Medley Race of 1981

At the 1981 Arcadia Invitational meet, I remember this was a race where the first-place team would get an award. In this case, it would be a gold Timex watch with the letters DM ARC INT. The letters stood for Distance Medley Arcadia Invitational. This distance-medley race was run in yards and would be converted to an adjusted meter time. It would have been 440-yard, 880-yard, 1,320-yard, and ends with a mile or a 1,760-yard race. Either way, it would have been converted to meters given the time.

This race was held on a Saturday evening, May 2, 1981, under the bright lights of the Arcadia Stadium. The distance medley was usually as follows: The first leg is the 440 run by me and is once around the track, the second leg is the 880 or two laps around the track, the third leg is 1,320 or three laps around the track, and the last leg is a mile, which is four laps around the track, 1,600 meters or 1,760 yards. The anchor would be the star and the Orange County champion in the mile. He, along with a sophomore, was also to be part of a meet record of 748.4 in the 3,200 or two-mile race, also setting himself as a state finalist.

I started the race in a staggered position with fourteen other schools. The first leg begins with me in the 400-meter leg. I got stuck in the pack in the seventh position and decided to step out of the pack around the 220-yard mark. I started with the 440-yard dash, and I felt the added pressure to secure the lead position. The crowd roared, and many would stand up. As I stepped out of the pack, I ran around seven others to take the lead. I stayed in the lead all the way to the first hand off. Before the turn before handing the baton to the man who bore my same last name, he ran the 880 and would stay in fourth position after my hand off. He got passed at the hand off. The 880 star would take the baton for the three-lap leg of this race. I felt fear and excitement at the same time. It seemed to motivate me enough to run my leg of the 440-yard dash in what I was told was a 48.7 split time, giving us the lead and only slightly ahead of the other runners. The runners had caught up to me at the baton-exchange. Our next runner was a trained distance runner. He also had the same last name as I have. He would now run the second leg of the race at 880 yards. As I handed the baton off, just a couple of runners had passed him. This was still very impressive, given the caliber of runners we were dealing with. I began to chase my teammate who was running the second leg of the race. I kept close to him, screaming, "Go! Go!" as I was in the center of the grass, running back and forth, straight across at midfield. He would maintain that spot. The normal star of the 880 runner was also a star runner at longer distances, such as the mile and two mile. He had been put in the third position at 1,320 yards. This was three laps around the track. He would catch up to the other runners and had moved into second place before his first lap had ended. By the second lap, he would battle for the first position on the subsequent second and third laps of this very competitive race with the Compton High School team. On the third lap, he would be about dead even before handing off to the senior star for the final leg at 1,760 yards or the mile. The first lap would immediately start a battle similar to a horse race with every lap.

This race was down to three teams: El Modena, Compton, and Camarillo. For the most part, it was really a two-man race as the El Modena runner and the Compton High runner would battle for first place. Camarillo was close enough to be a threat. The Compton anchor runner had already run a 413.85 in the mile that same day and won the mile race. However, he would stay even and battled for the lead for the first two laps of this distance-medley race.

I continued running straight across at midfield and yelling, "Go! Go!" and would continue up until the second lap of the final leg of the race. My track mates told me to stop running after them. I had run out of gas bigtime anyway and still screamed from afar.

The race with these anchors would go back and forth, changing positions constantly by as much as two yards in each lap of this most exciting race. I honestly had never seen a closer battle up until this point. Here, we are all battling to win. I thought we might finish second, and then our senior anchor would get the extra energy with an unbelievable kick and win by about two yards, with a time of 10:15 06, Compton in second with a time of 10:15 13, Camarillo took third with a 10:15 80, and fourth was close to five seconds behind with a time of 10:19 59. The crowd was astonished and in disbelief. Many local teams and fans had wanted the Compton team to win.

The Compton fans started shouting, "Noooooooo!"

However, ElMo's distance-medley team had not only won the race, but also set an Orange County record, with a time of 10:15.06, for 1981.

One thing I know for sure is this was the most exciting race I had ever been a witness to. I was proud to be a part of this historic race. The Orange County record was broken in 1987 by Corona Del Mar but still remains one of the fastest times of all Orange County schools. Our four-man team would be invited to a dinner and award at the Orange Elks Lodge just past the circle heading east located in Orange.

The Elks Lodge began to tell us of other athletes who had been invited to the lodge. I would learn there that someone I had a class with at Portola Junior High with had just passed away. He had, at ninth grade, passed his GED and began his career as a horse jockey. He had dedicated himself to something he loved, but sadly, he died in a horse accident on April 18, 1981. He was just seventeen years old.

We would be given a special award for what we had accomplished in the distance-medley race.

22

CHAPTER

In Summary, 1981 Track

Our track sprinters took first in the 440-yard relay and first in the mile relay at the Century League championships. I took first in the 220 and 440 at the Century League championships. We took first in the varsity 4x110 and 4x220 and a second place in the mile relay at the Orange Unified Rotary Relays. We took two medals at the prestigious Mt. Sac Invitational. One would include a second-place finish in the mile relay. We also took the Arcadia Invitational distance-medley relay, setting an Orange County record, which stood for five years. We were invited to the Orange Elks Lodge and received an award for the latter accomplishment.

I would receive other awards and four plaques at El Modena's awards ceremony, two of which included high point man and most inspirational. The star senior distance runner would be the MVP of the El Modena track squad, placing first in the mile at the OC championships, part of a meet record in the 3,200m relay, a state finalist in the 2-mile, as well as many other accomplishments I am quite sure.

Next year, the three juniors would become seniors, and the two sophomores would continue breaking records and getting better every year, always outdoing what they had previously accomplished. My sprint coach wrote in my yearbook, and I quote, "You've got what it takes—lots of guts and desire. You're my type of people. You did a great job as an individual and a team trackster. I've really enjoyed being your coach. Stay in shape and run in the summer meets, okay? Let's see about a 47.4 (440) 21.8 220 and a 9.7 100. That's a realistic goal for you. Good luck sincerely." I just read this in 2020.

23
CHAPTER

El Modena Track 1982 Track Personalities

This is our senior year for the star football running back and sprinter, my fellow sprinter friend and myself. My fellow seniors had taken to partying and comedy to the extreme. The star football player had The Blur written on his white 1962 Plymouth Valiant. With his speed, it was the appropriate name. He never minded doing anything that was spirited or party-like. He used to call me scissor face, as a way to describe my lack of shaving correctly. This, in fact, would stick with others and be added as a nickname to my beloved Hype Squad shirt. This was a club similar to a pep squad of guys who partied together. We showed up as a cheer squad at football games as well as instigating ways to create havoc to other schools. For example, Villa Park High was known as the "Weenies on the Hill" and Orange High, well, Oranges, of course. Legend would have it that others had put Weenies and Oranges in these school pools. I only was at one of the events as I generally could not go out on school nights. There were probably fifteen of us guys. Someone had the big idea of stealing little foam bean bag balls from a company called Marco in Tustin, California, and scattering them all over Foothill High School. I only watched from afar. The whole school was almost immediately surrounded with police officers. Somehow myself and one other guy were the only ones not arrested. Rumor has it that the first guy caught would "snitch" on the rest of the Hype Squad. The guys were required to work at the business to pay for the stolen merchandise. Maybe they did not know we came. We heard that the Foothill freshmen were the ones to clean the school mess up.

Meanwhile, track practice had already begun our final season. My sprinter friend had Neuby on his Hype Squad shirt and his mini truck. He is the one who would shout a long "AHHHHH" and increase his sound higher and higher for as long as he could and then had a smile and laugh that I can still remember. He, I am told, had also not participated in the

Foothill High theasical. He could also be seen pulling down his track shorts and running awkwardly out to track practice a couple of times. The sprint coach would then say in a serious but allowable way, "Quit your dicking around."

This was the year we partied like crazy nuts, but generally, our track squad would win our Century League events, placing first, second, and third. This generally included the 100-yard, 220-yard, 440-yard, 440-yard relay, and the mile relay races with the exception of perhaps visits by our SAV and OHS rivals.

I still had periodic problems with my diabetes, working, periodic smoking and drinking, etc. What is ironic is I started losing in the 100. I only got better at the 220, 440, and mile relay. Sometimes when ElMo got out on a minimum day, someone would throw a party, which were usually referred to as nooners. These parties would include playing drinking games such as quarters. This for those who don't know, it would be where you may bounce a quarter in a cup, and if you missed getting the quarter to bounce into the cup, the person bouncing would have to drink. If you made it into the cup, you could choose anyone else in the room to drink the beer already poured in the cup. People may have also smoked pot.

Sometimes we may have a track meet on a minimum day and have to return to school for it like two or three hours later. This was the case after a nooner for the meet against Tustin High School in 1982. I had partied but thought no problem, they are the last place team, and don't have to worry about it. However, what we didn't know was the *Orange County Register* newspaper was there and took a shot of us running the 100. We, indeed, won the race with first-, second-, third-, and fourth-place wins. I was drunk and barely got a debatable third. In the *Register* photo, maybe you can tell.

We had heats of a race. The junior varsity would race first, and I was waiting for the 220, and I had to urinate very badly as my sugars were probably high. I actually stood behind someone, turned around, and I sneaked out to pee. I was within sight of the referee who started the races. A couple of guys were laughing, saying, "You're gonna get caught."

Luckily, I got away with it and still won my 220-yard race. Maybe it was the Missing Persons song "Mental Hopscotch" I heard while sprinting that inspired me.

24
CHAPTER

1982, My Final Season

I truly thought my account of our track squad for this year was going to be quite easy.

However, I have found some facts and print sources are conflicting or nonexistent.

My attempts on trying to prove every detail and jog the memories of my fellow mates are hazy at best. I have not wanted to sound conceited or act like I was in any way superior to my fellow sprinters.

I do have a favorite race of mine in 1982. It was the reason this book was called *From Last to First*. One of our coaches entered us in the sprint medley. Our cross-country coach entered us in this race and had to lie about our time by one-tenth of a second. This was to be ranked last or fifteenth place just to run this race. Yet we were up for the challenge.

The Humble Star Runner runs a 220 and hands it off to the Comedian who runs another 220. I run a 440-yard and Neuby hands it off to me and yells, "Go!"

I would run the 440-yard dash as fast as I ever had to hand off to the 880-yard dash star. He would fly to help us have the fastest time in the nation for 1982. It was only a week before two teams from New York broke it.

We received a letter from our principal that we had run the sprint medley the fastest time in the nation for 1982.

25

CHAPTER

The debate, which is better, Arcadia Invitational or Mt. Sac Invitational? I have texted the two juniors from our former relay team. The star 880 runner said he did not know and that both were competitive. The Humble Star stated he thought Mt. Sac was a little better, and originally, I had thought the same thing. I mean, how could you argue with that with catch phrases, such as "Home to the World's Best Athletes" and medals with "One Step to the Olympics" written on them? Arcadia has their catch phrase "Home to National Records" and now boasts the largest meet and having the most athletes in the country.

I then read the history of the meets. The Mt. Sac Relays started in 1959 and have always been run in Walnut, California, usually mid-April, while the Arcadia Invitational was generally run a week later. In our case, on Saturday, May 2, 1982. the Mt. Sac Invitational could be run day or night. However, we ran our mile relay in the evening. The Arcadia Invitational was definitely run in the evening as with our sprint medley. At the Mt. Sac Relays, there were college and future Olympian runners. This meet seemed to be a prelude to the future games of the Olympics, perhaps hence the phrases associated with this meet. The Arcadia Invitational states it has twenty-five national high school records and helped produce 152 Olympians. So if we are considering only high schools, I might say Arcadia because it is dedicated to the best high school athletes. Mt. Sac would be high school, college, and future Olympians. I still think I would have to choose Mt. Sac as the track would seem better and faster. The same schools seemed to have a lot in common, with the same athletes at one time or another. The competition seemed to be the same. I still would say Mt. Sac only because of a slightly better track. As far as times in high school, I truly find the race times to have been similar and have not found a single race for exact comparison to prove one venue better than the other for high school races.

26

CHAPTER

The Worst Decision I Made in 1982

I hesitated to write about this part of my life. If this may save someone, so be it. About midyear, our school had an assembly, and our school would end on a minimum day afterward. A blond-headed surfer-type guy asked me if I wanted to go over to his house instead of the assembly. He said we would listen to music and that he lived close by. I agreed, and when I got to his home, he, indeed, started playing music. By about the third song, he pulled out a small mirror, and I saw two lines of what looked almost like baby powder on the mirror. He offered me one. I figured it was super bad for you and a drug that would hurt me very badly. He kept offering the line to me several times and assured me it would not hurt me. I unfortunately finally agreed. Instantly, I felt extremely happy and asked if he had more. This was actually cocaine. He said no, that was all he had. I would find out he actually sold this sometimes. I never did this with him again. However, there were many sources and supplies circulating in high schools in the '80s. I then would do this sometimes when I had the chance. It seemed to be a way of coping with my unhappiness off the track. This was a rich man's drug that was in abundance. I would quickly find that you had to do more and more to feel the effect I experienced the first time I did this. The high quickly dissipated. Many high schoolers had fallen prey to this drug. This drug would become a source of communication and promiscuity. This drug always left you wanting more. If you had more, you would get sicker and sicker with the effects of it wearing off. I still can remember the good feeling and the extreme sick feelings coming off it if you had too much. I do not believe it is really worth the risk. I do not think it was worth the trade-offs.

27
CHAPTER

The Races Ran

My races had started to become the 220, 440, 440 relay, and the mile Relays. As far as the Century League that we were in, our track squad pretty much dominated the relays, and I would generally win most of my 220 and 440 races. I always anchored the relays in the league. There was a time I remember when we were behind in a league race by quite a bit, and a couple of guys were saying, "Look he is tired."

I angrily replied, "Bullshit," and caught up to the guy and won the race.

There were more races similar to the latter. We generally won our races in the 440 relay, and the mile relay. I would take first or second in the 220 and first in the 440-yard dash all season. My fellow sprinters would take care of the 100-yard dash and the hurdles also most of the time during the Century League season. At the Orange County championships, our junior star 880 runner would take first place with a time of 156.30. Our Humble Star would place first in the triple jump with an amazing jump of 46 8 ½. Our track-and-field team would take second in these OC championships, thanks probably to the longer distances and field events. We would take first place in the 440-yard relay but in an invitational listed with the same name as the OC championships. I took first place in the 440-yard dash in an invitational listed as the OC championships. We also took second in the OC invite championships mile relay.

The cross-country and track coach decided to enter the sprinters in a series of prestigious invitational events, the first being Mt. Sac Invitational with our mile-relay team. This particular race was run at night under the stadium lights, and I would be placed in second position. The race began with a junior who had the last name that was used as another name for a *galloping horse* running. He was similar to the Humble Star, except he was shorter and maybe slightly more outspoken. He would run his fastest quarter to date. He ran a very fast first leg, and we took a second-place finish according to the medal received.

We were many in competition with our nemesis Santa Ana Valley High. For every competition, you are given a point system on the place you take in any given track-and-field event. First place, your team gets five points, for second place three points, and third place one point. This was a good year for our sprinters. The points were with one race or field event of each other with Valley.

We won the varsity 440 relay and the mile relay. Santa Ana Valley would take the long jump and perhaps other events like the shot put. I was able to win my 440 and somehow took the 220. Then we would need only one point to clench the Century League championships.

It seemed like we were going to win a very tight championship. But The Blur, the star running back and sprinter hurdler, was unable to race. The replacement hurdler was going to need a third place as we were far enough ahead in points. This was one of Valley's strong races. Unfortunately, the junior runner had not placed, and we ended up taking second place, losing the Century League championships by just one point.

The following weekend were CIF qualifiers races. We qualified with our mile-relay team. All that was left was for me to be able to qualify in the 440-yard dash. Two of us quarter-milers were undefeated in the 440. He was a gentleman from Canyon High School. We had never run against each other. His letterman's jacket said "Quarterhorse" on the back of it. I had heard of this and decided to have "Beetlebomb" stitched on the back of mine. This was a song about a racehorse I had heard on the Dr. Demento show. His show was the best for humorous songs. This particular song talks about a horse that is dead last in a race and remains that way all the way down to the final stretch of the race. Throughout the song, it says the name of this horse as if it had no chance to win whatsoever. But Bettlebomb slowly catches up, and with a cloud of smoke, it is "BeetleBomb" who wins the race. I would be in lane 5 and the Canyon High runner in lane 4. We were confident the race was going to be between us two. However, I never doubted anyone's ability to take a race. The runners all lined up, and I started to get in my blocks. The Canyon guy said, "Wait, wait," started rubbing one of his eyes, and said, "I lost my contact."

I started helping him look on the ground for the said missing contact. I remember I said to him, "If you're not going to race, then I won't."

He then stated that it was in his eye all along. I instantly thought that he may have wanted to psych me out. This made me more determined to win the race. We lined up for the final of the 440-yard dash. "On your marks, set," and the gun goes off.

This was going to be the hardest race of the season. We remained close throughout the race, but on the last turn, I had a kick and was able to take him by just a few yards.

28

CHAPTER

The Record-Setting Sprint Relay

The cross-country coach told us we had to lie by 1/10th of a second to be ranked last or fifteenth to enter the Arcadia Invitational's relay. This race consisted of the Humble Star running his fastest time. His first was a 200. He rockets out of the blocks, hands off to the Comedian Star, who runs his best 200 to date. He handed it off to me, and I would have a great 440 split time. The 880 star would run the fastest I had seen him run, and apparently, we had taken first in the nation in the sprint medley at the Arcadia Invitational with a time of 327.33. But we would soon hear that a team from Brooklyn, New York, had beaten that time a week later. With a time of 327.2 with the team's second and third, making us third in the United States overall. But alas, a team from Baytown Sterling in Texas had broken that time, with a time of 323.3, making us actually fourth in the United States in 1982 according to my records. This also has us fifth of all time in Orange County schools in California. We had also placed third in the 440-yard relay. The 440-yard relay would probably have included El Modena's star football running back. We would enter an Orange County relay meet called the Rotary Relays. We took first place in the 4x110, the 4x220, and the 4x400. These medals are nice and have stood the test of time with little to no oxidation. On May 23, 1982, we entered the Sunkist Invitational. This event took place at the LA Sports Arena. This race took place indoors on a banked wooden track. It kind of made you spring up when you ran on it. It was too difficult to control for us. We had no warm-up on this difficult track and did not even place but still ran a decent race in this mile relay. Though there were probably other competitions we may have entered, I can only account for two more: Century League championships and CIF. I have believed this for years and years. The cross-country coach is still living in Orange.

29

CHAPTER

CIF Prelims 1982

This is the only time I remember racing in the CIF meet, though I had made CIF all three years of high school. I would race with my fellow sprinters in the mile relay as well as myself racing in the 440-yard dash. My former Orange High School coach came to cheer me on as he still had the fastest time in the state in the 440-yard. The record was held for thirty years thus far in the Orange Unified School Division. I had already had a split, which would have broken his record. He briefly tells me good luck before the race. I felt something was different. The caliber of runners were unlike anything I had ever seen before. I still felt like I had a chance to win the race. When it came time for the lane assignments, I was in the farthest outside lane or the ninth position. I had always run catch up and never staggered ahead before. I had always run in lane 4 or 5. But I was already psyching myself out. I would need either first or second or the fastest third-place time to make it to qualify for the finals. We enter our blocks. The gun goes off, and I act like it is a 100-yard dash once again, running as fast as I could. I am constantly hearing my name being called out over the PA system, saying very quickly my name in lane 9, and I was feeling, "Hey, I am gonna take this thing!"

I am quite a length ahead until the last turn. Then all of a sudden, three of the runners had taken me from the inside on the final turn and passed me. At the end of the turn, I had hit a wall and was in fourth place, unable to catch the runners, and I was barely able to finish the race. I had not qualified to run, and my season was over as an individual sprinter. The mile relay would be run about an hour later. I do not have any memory of the actual race. I was so upset for not making the finals that I had selfishly not cared who anchored the mile relay, and the 880-meter star would take the helm.

Almost always, I anchored the mile-relay races. What I do remember is our heat. We took sixth place overall. This had given us a medal, but alas, we had not qualified for the masters qualification meet. This was at Cerritos College on May 27, 1982. The state meet would be held on June 4 and 5 at Hughes Stadium in Sacramento, California. The junior Humble Star and the junior star in the 800 had wanted to go to this meet. Nueby and I had decided we would not be participating if we had qualified in either the state prelims meet or state meet as it was the same weekend as El Modena's senior prom. We had girlfriends, and we had plans to party. We did not want to disappoint our girlfriends, and many of us had rented limos for the prom. We really did not think we really had any chance to place in either meets. We wanted to party, and we had enough to reflect on in the years we had spent running track.

We still had the Century League championships where I would defend my 440- and 220-yard races. This was different as my 440 race would have me against another undefeated quarter-miler from Canyon High School. I had already won the 220.

Our mile relay team of the Galloping Horse, the Comedian, the 880 Star, and myself would take the mile-relay Century League champion title as well as the 440-yard relay.

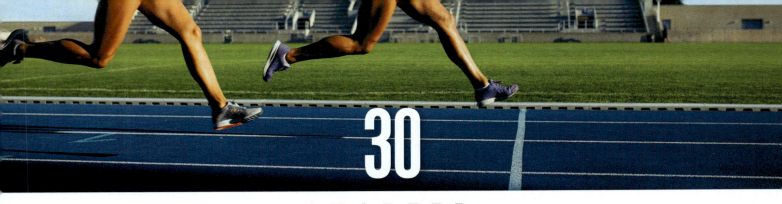

30

CHAPTER

We earned first place in the 440 and mile relays in the Century League championships. At the OC Invitational championships, our 440-yard relay took first place with a time of 43.1. I took first in the 440-yard dash at the same event. My fellow sprinters also took second in the mile relay at the Mt. Sac Relays. We took first place in the sprint medley, setting a national record at the Mt. San Antonio relays. Additionally, we additionally had a sixth-place finish in the CIF prelims in the mile relay. This probably was only a portion of the awards we all earned, but hey, it has been over forty years ago. Last I checked, the 800 Star is still listed in the CIF record books for the 880. He placed first and ran a 156.30 at the OC championships. The Humble Star, as of the time of writing this, still holds the high school record. At the Orange County championships, he took first place with the awesome jump of 46 8 ½. The sophomore, whose name was that of a type of horse, was the first leg of our high school mile-relay record team. He also ran at various times in the other relay races. The Blur was very quick in the hurdles and as part of some of our quickest 440-relay races. "Neuby," a.k.a. "the Comedian," won many 100-yard dash races, ran the 220, and played an integral part of the mile relays. He was also on the first-place sprint-medley-race team at the Mt. Sac Invitational. Our sprint-medley relay would hold for a short time to be the fastest in the nation with a time of 327.33. I found this project to be extremely difficult. I decided from the beginning to not use the names of my fellow track squads. They will know who they are by what I have written. I have some of my pictures, awards, and personally printed material that I own to serve as reminders of my fellow athletes. There are a lot of "could have," "should have," "would have." For me, I feel reflected on this writing. I often wonder how much better we might have fared if we had been in a four-year high school instead of a three-year one. It also seems the tracks are better today. We often ran our races on dirt tracks. Then again looking back to the past record times that took several years to break even given the newer tracks.

I will tell you now, my name is Robert Smith a.k.a. Rob or Robbie.

Two of the three junior sprinters would have a more than stellar track season in 1983. For just one example, the 880 Star had become the CIF Southern Section Champion in the 880 race. This, I believe, was held at Cerritos College in California. This would also be prior to the state final held in June at Hughes Stadium in Sacramento, California. They had surpassed our accomplishments as individuals. They would also have success in college running track times I only had dreamed about. Were we the best? No. I do still believe that for the time, there is a great debate on who had the most fun. We represented the Southern Section with pride. For track in the '70s and '80s, I truly still feel a kinship with all our competitors of that time. The track members who were closest to me were a bunch of crazy kids having fun and enjoying the competition. Most of all, we still are friends to this day, I hope, and that still means the world to me.

31
CHAPTER

After Graduation 1982

The mother of one of the Hype Squad guys had worked for a travel agency. He had offered several young men if we wanted to celebrate our graduation in Waikiki, Hawaii. He also loved to party, and we had past travels, such as driving to a Big Bear cabin. This was just about ten of us guys. We spent the weekend drinking and smoking cigars. The Hawaii trip he had organized would be for a week including a hotel. The hotel was going to be right on the sand at a cost, I believe, just shy of $600. After some convincing, my mother agreed to pay for my trip as a graduation gift if I would work for my spending money.

During my time at El Modena, I did not have a counselor who would probe me for any future plans to attend college. I did not have the necessary classes that would be required to attend a university. However, my mom had promised, if I could get into college, she would provide a way to pay for it. I did not trust this to be true. However, a man I knew was also going to be in Hawaii at the same time as my friends. I was loving the beauty and fun I was having in Hawaii. My friend offered to get information and apply to the University of Hawaii. He did as he promised, and as soon as I got the book and application, I briefly looked at it and then with some excitement, carefully entered the information I received back into one of my suitcases.

We had a "blast" in Waikiki, and I was dreaming of the time I might return and possibly go to college there. When I returned home, I presented the information about college to my mother, who quickly said, "Hawaii, I am so sure."

I was hurt but knew we did not have much money, and besides, I did not exactly have a plan. My parents and I had not really discussed any type of real college plans. I did not have the best grades or even enough of the classes to get in.

A day or two later, I received a letter by mail from the University of Santa Barbara. The letter congratulated me on some of the success I had running track. The letter then asked me to enter my grades in such classes as chemistry, and I really did not have any of the classes they asked for. I continued some of my partying ways and taking jobs and giving some sort of payment to continue living at home.

Another couple of days later, I received a letter from Orange Coast Junior College in Costa Mesa, California. It stated they had a good track program and invited me to go out for track. I decided to attend Orange Coast. I had no idea I would have been able to get my AA degree and possibly transfer to a university if I did not have enough money or plan to enter college. I did not feel comfortable where I lived in Huntington Beach. I would take some classes then. However, time had gone by, and I felt I was no longer in a place I would be able to try out for any track team. I continued going to junior colleges but had let a time of bad choices get the best of me.

I guess, as Mom would say, I had no one to blame but myself.

Lampson Leopards Elementary School - Sixth-Grade Track

Cerro Villa Junior High versus Portola Junior High

The Cerro Villa Star and I

Laguna Beach Trophy Meet 1980

Sunkist Invitational LA Coliseum 1982
Me running the mile relay

Rob Smith, Steve Valen,
Craig Smith, Rubin Esparza.
Distance Medley Relay
Arcadia Invitational - 1981
First Place - 10:15.07!

April 29, 1982

Mr. Rob Smith
4423 E. Euclid
Orange, California   92669

Dear Rob:

Congratulations to you and the other members of your relay team for an outstanding performance at the 24th Annual Mt. San Antonio Relays. Mr. Weber and I are very proud of the team for running the fastest time of any relay team in the nation for 1982.

Thanks for a superb performance.

Sincerely,

John Ikerd

John Ikerd
Principal

JI/br

cc: Mr. Weber

1982 Record-Breaking Spring Medley Team